PRAISE FOR M. L. BUCHMAN

Top 10 Romance of 2012, 2015, and 2016.

— BOOKLIST: THE NIGHT IS MINE, HOT POINT,
HEART STRIKE

One of our favorite authors.

— RT BOOK REVIEWS

Buchman has catapulted his way to the top tier of my favorite authors.

— FRESH FICTION

A favorite author of mine. I'll read anything that carries his name, no questions asked. Meet your new favorite author!

— THE SASSY BOOKSTER, FLASH OF FIRE

M.L. Buchman is guaranteed to get me lost in a good story.

— THE READING CAFE, WAY OF THE WARRIOR:
NSDQ

I love Buchman's writing. His vivid descriptions bring
everything to life in an unforgettable way.

— PURE JONEL, HOT POINT

COPS AND FATHERS

A LANALEE PATTERSON STORY

M. L. BUCHMAN

Buchman Bookworks

Other works by M. L. Buchman:

The Night Stalkers

MAIN FLIGHT

The Night Is Mine
I Own the Dawn
Wait Until Dark
Take Over at Midnight
Light Up the Night
Bring On the Dusk
By Break of Day

WHITE HOUSE HOLIDAY

Daniel's Christmas
Frank's Independence Day
Peter's Christmas
Zachary's Christmas
Roy's Independence Day
Damien's Christmas

AND THE NAVY

Christmas at Steel Beach
Christmas at Peleliu Cove

5E

Target of the Heart
Target Lock on Love
Target of Mine

Firehawks

MAIN FLIGHT

Pure Heat
Full Blaze
Hot Point
Flash of Fire
Wild Fire

SMOKEJUMPERS

Wildfire at Dawn
Wildfire at Larch Creek
Wildfire on the Skagit

Delta Force

Target Engaged
Heart Strike
Wild Justice

White House Protection Force

Off the Leash
On Your Mark
In the Weeds

Where Dreams

Where Dreams are Born
Where Dreams Reside
Where Dreams Are of Christmas
Where Dreams Unfold
Where Dreams Are Written

Eagle Cove

Return to Eagle Cove
Recipe for Eagle Cove
Longing for Eagle Cove
Keepsake for Eagle Cove

Henderson's Ranch

Nathan's Big Sky
Big Sky, Loyal Heart

Love Abroad

Heart of the Cotswolds: England
Path of Love: Cinque Terre, Italy

Dead Chef Thrillers

Swap Out!
One Chef!
Two Chef!

Deities Anonymous

Cookbook from Hell: Reheated
Saviors 101

SF/F Titles

The Nara Reaction
Monk's Maze
the Me and Elsie Chronicles

Strategies for Success (NF)

Managing Your Inner Artist/Writer
Estate Planning for Authors

CHAPTER 1

It was well past sunrise when Lana rolled up to the building. An unimaginably long night, especially as she'd had a full day in front of it. Why she'd ever thought being a private eye would be easier than being a cop…

She throttled back but the thudding Harley still spooked most of the dog-walker's charges when she popped it up onto the sidewalk. As soon as she was over the curb, she cut the engine, but it gave a final bang that panicked Marcus' dogs, tangling him in their leashes. She rolled the bike against her building's facade. Parking on the sidewalk on Commonwealth Ave. in the heart of Boston should have gotten her a whole string of tickets, but the old brownstone had a small bay—left over from when it had been a horse-and-buggy fire station before they'd bricked it in and condoed it—that fit her bike perfectly. It was one of her favorite stealth parking spots in the city.

"Damn it, Lana!" by some miracle, Marcus had managed to remain upright despite being wrapped up like *The Mummy* in various DayGlo leash colors.

"It's a good thing the dogs are all pulling in different

directions, or you'd be faceplanted on the concrete." She kicked the stand down and used the yellow brick wall to steady herself as she swung off the bike. It was a good thing it was the only yellow one in the block of red brick buildings, otherwise she'd have been too tired to find it and might have slept on a bench where the Comm. Ave. park split the street in two.

"Wouldn't be the first time," he growled as one of the dogs took advantage of his bound state to crotch him with its nose.

"Sorry, Marcus." One of the dogs finally broke free and bounded for her arms. Maximillian's abrupt departure unbalanced the forces and Marcus went down. The rest of the pack assumed it was playtime and buried the teen until little more than his shot of black hair showed through the melee. His frustrated laughs were the best sound she'd heard in a while.

Maximillian—never Max, he wouldn't answer to it and his owner wouldn't tolerate it—might only be a twenty-pound sheltie, but she was tired enough that his lunge knocked her to the sidewalk as well. The dumb dog began licking her faceplate free of bugs. She flipped up the visor and was rewarded with a string of buggy dog slime across her Ray-Bans and the bridge of her nose.

"Cut that out, you stupid animal."

Marcus was slowly sorting himself out. "Serves you right."

"You inbound or out?" She still had to shout to be heard over the pack who wanted to play some more.

"Inbound, Patterson. Some Private Eye you are, can't even tell when a man is done for the morning. You wanna take Maximilian up?"

"Got it covered. So how's the dog-walking doing for ya?" She finally forced the sheltie down onto four legs on the ground, like any decent dog, and unclipped the leash that had slipped out of Marcus' hand. Keeping Maximillian close wasn't the issue. Actually walking while he did his best to hug her ankles was the challenge with him.

"Except for someone on their noisy, fart-blasting machine, it's great. I'm gonna try to get Keith out of the gang to give me a hand. I've got more offers to walk than I can handle. Tips help, too, you know."

"No way, me Bucko. I'm sure you scalped The Judge already on the way out. We both know she's a soft touch when it comes to her dog."

His broad grin lit up his face, "Can't blame a guy for trying."

"The fact that you're trying, that's the good bit...Keith, hunh. Why him?"

"He's okay." Marcus unwrapped a cocker spaniel's leash from about his neck before the dog could throttle him.

Lana thought about his choice, it was a good one. Most of the boys were too far gone into the gang culture, but Keith was okay, always on the fringe of the worst of it. She'd broken Marcus loose with a quick bike trip over to the state pen. They'd even been there in time for a max security transfer—two of the damn scariest brutes she'd ever seen. If he could rescue another one on his own, it would be that much less for her to do.

Finally unsnarled of two poodles, a Golden Retriever (though whatever idiot had one of those in the city should be shot), three mutts, and an elegant Afghan Hound, Marcus waved and headed for his next drop-off down the Ave.

Maximillian spent more time tripping her than walking as she staggered up the front steps. Leaning her head against the brick, she keyed in the security codes. After the third "buzz" of failure, she dragged off her leather glove and tried again. Only took two attempts barehanded. Click and snap and she was into the lobby. White, clean, dark marble floor, it smelled of pine-cleaner and money. So counter to the rest of her night that it was beyond strange and off into surreal.

Thank god the elevator was open and waiting, she plunged in and punched for the fifth floor. Her helmet tried to rip the ears off the side of her head as she dragged it clear. If there was an inch of her that wasn't sore, her body wasn't informing her about it.

She staggered to the front door.

Where were her keys? She opened her hand and all she held was a folded-up leash. They must be down in the bike. Nope! No way she was going back down. Let them steal the beast of a machine—she'd buy a nice light Kawasaki crotch rocket next time, a real street bike. She stuffed the leash into her helmet, leaned her head against the door, and pounded on it with the side of her fist.

The Sheltie, dying to be in on the game, raced up and down the pristine hall, nails clacking brightly on the marble tile and barking loudly enough to roust everyone in all four apartments on her floor—and probably those above and below.

She was just summoning the energy to yell at the animal when the door latch clicked. With her weight against it, the door flew open and she tumbled inward, landing hard against the white entry carpet. Her helmet clattered and rolled to a stop against a pair of leather loafers. Sharp little paws instantly trotted across her back and legs like a masseuse on drugs—bad ones. Once again conveniently at floor level, her ear was slathered in dog slime before he tried to launch upward using the aching remains of her shoulders as a launching pad.

"Hi, Maximillian."

Lana sometimes wondered who was more important to Verna, Max or herself. She claimed that the dog wouldn't understand if it wasn't greeted first, whereas she, a grown woman, really ought to.

"Good morning, Lana. And what kind of trouble did you get into last night? Anything to land you in my court?"

Lana rolled onto her back and looked up the long, sharp crease of Verna's pale blue Armani pantsuit. Judge Verna was always impeccable, even though she'd be shrouded in dark robes throughout the day.

"Probably. But three kids are safe now in their grandparents' care—who are sick of their son and daughter-in-law. The mother's in detox, a little worse for wear, not my doing. The father, perhaps under duress, attended four different AA meetings in a row in different parts of the city before Sergeant Thompson was kind enough to toss him in the can for me, much worse for the wear. I won't deny that was my doing. You'll probably have a chance to meet him today on child abuse charges. If he claims I roughed him up, the answer is yes. If he claims I robbed him, I gave every cent, plus some of your hard earned money to the grandparents for one-way tickets out of town. Do me a favor?"

Verna widened her dark eyes just enough to ask the question without speaking as she looked down from on high.

"Bring back the death penalty and erase this guy. Three-time offender. A complete shit."

"Are you intending to lounge there across the threshold all day, or are you going to drag those long legs in and actually stay for a while?"

"Guess I could stay for a bit," she pushed up to kneeling position and waited for her head to stop spinning.

That line had become a thing between them; as deep as a kiss and as intimate as a caress.

She'd known Judge Verna Carlisle for a while—from the other side of the bench, though not the *wrong* side, not too often anyway—when The Judge had asked her to stay after the last docket of the day. A friendly chat in chambers. Dinner—in a much nicer place than was Lana's norm. A few drinks—less than her norm. Then…

Lana had never gone home with a woman before, but there was something about Verna Carlisle that drew her in. The sex had been a major eye-opener. But when she'd tried to slip away somewhere past oh-dark-thirty, Verna had leveled that judge's voice at her with just enough heat.

"Why don't you stay for a while?" The heat that lay behind that cool exterior had proved irresistible.

"Guess I could stay for a bit," she'd confessed before slipping back between the sheets and into The Judge's arms. That same line had her staying 'til dawn, toothbrush and a change of clothes within a month, and moving in after six.

Lana used the doorknob to pull herself to her feet and kicked off her bike boots. Maximillian stuck his nose—a high connoisseur of stench—in one until much of his head was gone from view. She made a step toward the kitchen, but Verna's gaze stopped her cold. The woman could freeze steam with a glance. She turned back for her boots, shoving Maximillian aside to get them. Cracking open the closet door, she heaved them in. The worn black cowboy boots knocked against the neat rows of Verna's pumps, joggers, and loafers, scattering them about. She shoved the door closed; fix it after The Judge was gone.

Verna leaned in and placed a smooth, warm hand on her cheek. Her dark eyes could also melt steel. Her perfectly manicured nails, with their sensible clear polish, slid along Lana's neck and those muscles, at least, relaxed.

"Nice to see you, too."

Her kiss was long and sensuous, Lana wanted to reach for her but didn't want to mess up her perfect suit either. She landed back against the closet door as her knees threatened to go out from under her.

Then Verna's warmth and soft mouth were gone. Lana opened her eyes in time to see her check that her shoulder-length brown hair still fell in that one smooth wave that suited her patrician face so well.

"See you for dinner, and don't forget to pick up your father." In the faintest puff of lavender soap and a sky-blue pant suit, she was gone. Except for the roundhouse kick she'd just laid straight to the gut.

Pop.

Shit!

Lana had managed to forget. And that was not a bad feeling at all.

She slouched into the kitchen and jerked open the fridge. As she reached for the OJ, the leash and then her traitorously elusive keys fell from her hand onto the floor with a clatter that brought Max trotting over to investigate. She slugged back the crisp, cold liquid. It roared down her throat clearing away the putrid taste of that rattrap on West Elm and the sharp scent of blood she'd wiped from the little girl's legs. It cleared away the sickly sweet Thunderbird wine on the mother's breath—uncaring bitch had probably watched.

Lana'd cleared out what little money the family had stashed, including the drug-wad from down the front of the father's pants, and gave it to the grandparents to help them move away without a forwarding address. They'd agreed eagerly and would be gone before the end of the day. No damaged kid as evidence, so harder to nail the dad, but that was now Verna's problem.

Maybe she'd scared the Missus enough to nail her own husband to the wall.

If not, maybe Lana would see that "child molester" was whispered to his cellmates, not a popular profession behind bars. Maybe she'd do that anyway—The Judge wasn't the only one who knew how to give out a sentence.

She finished the OJ and tossed the pitcher into the sink where it bounced about before settling. She tried to jerk open the freezer to pull out another can—Verna hated when the next one wasn't thawed—but at the moment the handle was stronger than she was. That particular defeat she could hand and she staggered away toward the bathroom. She'd feel better with a shower, better able to face the one man she had nothing to say to.

She dropped her leather jacket somewhere near the front closet. Her tee-shirt, "Stop Plate Tectonics," lay crumpled in the hall. She had to sit on the bed to shuck off her riding leathers. That was the mistake. The bed was soft against her sore behind, clean, neatly made, it was everything that was Verna. The elegant quilt with its simple geometry and perfect choice of red, yellow, gray, and black made the "Amish Hearth" too cozy to resist.

She flopped back, struggled for a moment to pull the scrunchie from her long ponytail, and let sleep take her.

CHAPTER 2

ana woke in a pool of sunshine and a long, soft warmth along her leg. She reached for Verna and found an empty pillow. Maximillian gave her a love bite on her toes where he lounged against her. Verna never let him up on the bed, but he always played the odds with Lana.

"You've got my number, don't you?"

He sighed happily.

The phone rang again, at least she assumed it was again. She'd found it by the next ring and shoved it against her ear.

"Remember your father." Verna's voice breathed in her ear. "And remember to pick up your clothes."

"Go stick your head in a bucket, Judge."

"Sure, if you'll wash my hair."

"Love you, too. Thanks." That had taken her another six months past moving in to learn how to say. Another two years of practice hadn't made it any less incredible to say or to hear. The next step past that was looming, they'd even talked about it—or at least Verna had. Verna's home state of Vermont had instituted civil unions. There was a question

Lana would never be ready to answer in any way that would turn out good so she kept her mouth shut during those conversations.

Verna clicked off before Lana even moved the phone from her ear. She dropped it back in the cradle and sat up to give Maximillian a good belly rub.

"You and me buddy. The judge broke us both to the leash." When she found the spot that made his back leg really flail, she scritched it as well as she could with her chewed-off and broken fingernails.

A shower. She definitely needed a shower. A quick glance at the clock and she knew she was in trouble. His flight was hitting Logan at four, unless she was lucky and it hit the Charles River at 3:59.

She just had time to catch the T—ride the underground out to Logan Airport. But not with a shower. She lifted one arm and had her answer. Maximillian's freezing-cold nose, that was a magnet for all the worst smells on the planet, came over to investigate. She shoved him over so that he flopped onto Verna's side of the bed.

Ride the T, or shower and take the bike. Her pop would appreciate the former, but only if she and her stench rode in a separate car. She kicked the leathers under the bed as she moved for the shower. The plush carpet was the same color as Verna's pant-suit. With anyone else that would have been coincidence, but with The Judge she never knew.

CHAPTER 3

*L*ana swung the bike into the right lane, it was moving a *little* faster. Damn the man! Who on this planet ever had a flight arrive early. She roared through a narrow gap and slalomed her way up the highway's dotted line. Only when the lights flashed on in her rearview did she notice she'd blown past the marked cruiser, blue and white, bubble gum-machine light bar on the roof, and all.

Fishing down between her helmet and back collar, she yanked her long hair free and let it fly like a blond banner in the wind. The lights died and she heard Patrolman Jackson's voice on the PA over the roar of rush hour on Storrow Drive.

"Damn it, Lana. Drive with your eyes open next time."

She waved the Vulcan greeting in acknowledgement— hurray for fellow Trekkies—then laid back into the throttle leaving him far behind. He popped the siren at her but made no attempt to chase. She'd owe him a box of cookies or something, but the Old Man's plane would be landing at any moment.

Coming out of the tunnel, she was on the wrong side for the airport ramp so she goosed it and nearly clipped the nose of some yuppie in a new Beetle: the rare, extra-expensive yellow model. Why someone would pay extra money to drive around in a urine-colored car was beyond belief. It even had the custom-imported yellow tires. Shit, it must be nice to have money.

The Friday afternoon traffic was thick and nasty. Businessmen skipping for planes home, housewives scrambling to shop. Why didn't they all just go away so she could pick up her goddamn father, and spend a whole goddamn week with him having no idea what the hell to say? Three years in a row she'd traveled down to Florida. They'd hit the gym, gone deep sea fishing, and watch endless games on TV. They didn't talk. That wasn't going to work so well here.

Verna had promised to help, but even with the queen of charm in full mama-bear mode, it still wasn't going to be pretty.

He was waiting at the curb with a carry-on and a suiter. Shit, she'd forgotten about the luggage. Maybe he hadn't spotted her and she could just cruise on by. Even at seventy-five there was nothing wrong with his ex-cop, bullet-sharp eyesight. He picked her out before she was within a hundred feet. She rolled into the no-parking strip reserved for cabs and buses, the rest was a crowded mess.

Even as the Harley thudded to a stop, he rolled over in that broad-chested waddle of his as if his soul was too powerful to fit in a body that had spent forty-five years patrolling the streets. Ten years retired to Florida and he was still pure Force—always a capital letter with Pop, habit she'd picked up as well—with no signs of slowing down except for silver hair and wrinkles. Boston cop through and through.

"Hi, Pop."

"Interesting machine you have there, Lanalee." He always used her full name, even her driver's license didn't do that anymore. The slightest move of his eyebrow encompassed his bags and her chosen mode of transportation.

Couldn't the bastard even say hello?

"Yeah. I screwed up. Late night and all. We can stuff the carry-on into one of saddlebags and the suiter might fit in the other." She'd remembered the spare helmet—big enough to fit even his head—but she got no points for that either.

After a bit of painful, silent negotiation, the carry-on was split between the two saddlebags then tied empty to the short sissy bar. His Ruger Speed-Six 9mm service revolver shifted to his shoulder holster with a quick slight of hand that no untrained tourist would see despite standing next to him on the sidewalk. And his suits—probably all three that he owned but why he brought them only god could guess—were sandwiched between them. It wasn't as if they were going to any funerals this week.

His hands tapped uncertainly against her waist a few times before he settled them into tight fists around the sidebar seat holds.

"Ready?" she shouted back over her shoulder.

She took the low grumble of his chest against her back as an affirmative and swung out into traffic.

CHAPTER 4

"So, Davey, how did you and Lana's mother get together?"

She and Pop had met Verna at Yvonne's for a dinner so nice that even she herself enjoyed it—which wasn't like her. Fancy places usually freaked her out. She was more of a burger and brew gal, but Verna was always working to corrupt her. Now the three of them walked home together through the cool September evening.

Verna was unbelievable. She strolled along Commonwealth with her arm negligently through his with Lana trailing along in their wake, in total awe. Nobody, not even Mom had ever called Detective Sergeant David Patterson anything other than David. And he was smiling at her. Verna'd learned more about his life outside the Force tonight than Lana'd heard in the thirty-four years prior.

All of which made her feel like the teenage brat scuffing along through the maple leaves on the sidewalk. Scattered cars trickled past old, raggedy shops that dished out the best to trendy tourists. Now it was past dark, and

Commonwealth was left to the idle few strolling along under the historic streetlights. The Ave. had a parklike median down the center wide enough for a path, occasional benches, and enough grass for a picnic. The street ran to either side to service the line of historic brownstones. A couple were making out on a bench. Why couldn't she and Verna be doing that instead of—

"It's pretty funny actually," her father's voice was simultaneously gruff and mellow—the second part a big surprise. "Bernie, everyone called Bernice Bernie, was a flower-child and I was already twenty years in the Force. It was my luck that I got stuck with taking her into precinct after some protest. She leaned up against the screen in the back of my car and just starts chatting with me like we're sharing a box of donuts—not like she's handcuffed in the back of my cruiser. You know what?"

"No, what?" Verna put the proper amount of surprise in her voice which fooled none of them, but was perfect to the moment.

"We'd been through the same high school, and a lot of the same teachers, just most of twenty years apart." His affable rumble rose above the noise of a stoop party they were passing. A lot of the old buildings on Comm. Ave. had big sets of stone stairs, a common gathering place, even on cool evenings like this one. There were a couple of folk guitars, some of the people talked, others sang along. Bottles of beer and wine…she sighed. Not for her. Not tonight.

Her father's next words swirled to her on the backwash of wishful thinking.

"I didn't book her, of course. Never saw anything so beautiful in my life—Lanalee is her spitting image. She was conceived that night, or just before dawn the next morning." He pointed a short finger at a bench in the green median between Exeter and Fairfield. "Right there. On that bench."

"Pop! You never told me that." How could he? How could Mom have married someone so cold and so much older? Made love to him out in public like that? How…

Verna and Detective Sergeant David Patterson threw their heads back and laughed. It was like a Twilight Zone. The moment-after-the-Apocalypse impossible sorts of things suddenly started happening. Her father had warmth? He actually—

"Bernie was always a kick. God, that woman made me laugh. Right then said if we made a girl, she should be named for the girl Superman *should* have gone for, Lana Lang. She's the one who chose Lanalee."

Something else Lana had never known. Actually it was pretty cool. Maybe she should change her license back next time.

"Still miss her ever damn day—pardon my language, ma'am." It also explained why he still used her full name. A way to remember his dead wife, if not his daughter.

Mom had been murdered by a revenge rifle-shot through the bedroom window when Lana was ten—dead at twenty-nine. When Lana had moved into Verna's third floor brownstone condo, she'd made sure there was no roof angle on the bed and put in bullet-proof windows bedroom, bath, and living room one weekend when Verna was out of town to visit her parents.

She'd never heard her father laugh before tonight.

They all pulled to a halt before the code-locked door.

"This is our stop, Verna. Where may we escort you?"

"I live here as well."

"In the same building?

Verna glanced at her over his shoulder. Lana could feel her jaw open and shut. No sound escaped as the whirlpool swirled up inside to consume her brain in heat and fire. Judge Carlisle's eyes narrowed: accused, tried, condemned.

As her sentence was about to be pronounced, Lana managed to stammer it out.

"Verna and I are lovers, Pop. We live together in the same building, the same apartment…the same bed."

With the unstoppability of wrecking ball swinging to level a condemned district, Detective Sergeant David Patterson turned about until he faced her, and Verna was now the one behind his back. Verna's sharp nod said it was a damn good thing Lana had spoken up so fast. It also did nothing to belie the anger in her eyes.

Shit! Life was going along all roses until Pop showed up. How many boyfriends had run when they met him? How many high-school dates had *not* asked her to dance or had her home half-an-hour early to the formidable Detective Sergeant Patterson?

"When did this happen?"

"It's not something that 'happens', Pop. I just…like Verna. We're—"

"You're…what?"

"I'm—" the word still stuck in her throat. The people they socialized with, their friends, didn't need labels. Only parents needed labels. Goddamned, intolerant, old-fashio—

At the steps, a shadow moved behind her motorcycle. She leapt in front of Verna and dropped her weighted knife from her sleeve into her palm.

Out of the corner of her eye, she could see the cold glint of her father's stainless steel service revolver aimed at the heart of the shadow.

"Lana?"

It was little more than a whisper, a whisper she'd heard all too recently.

"Marcus?"

The shadow slumped a little. After a quick scan of the street, she slid her knife back up into the arm sheath.

"I made sure no one followed me," his voice came out slurred, barely a mumble. Not a good sign.

The sharp tang of blood cut through the chill fall air. She moved until she could place a hand on either arm, and helped him slide sideways, clear of the machine.

He hissed as she grasped his shoulder and would have dropped to the pavement if she hadn't caught him.

She shouted over her shoulder. "Verna, get the car. Pop go with her, make sure she's safe."

"I'm not a chil—"

Lana cut her off. "A beautiful woman in fancy rags is a target. Remember our deal. I take care of my shit and you stay clear of it. Now get the damn car."

The two of them hurried off, she could feel her father scanning the street even without turning to see them go.

"What happened, Marcus? I thought you were out of all that."

"I was." His breathing was little more than a wheeze as she gently probed the shoulder of his jacket. A knife slit crossed in from the arm but had caught on the heavy collar. Probably the only thing that had saved his jugular vein and his life. She turned him in the light and the entire front of his jeans jacket was black with blood.

"Or I thought I was." His voice was hazy.

Tire squeals behind her. The high thin whine of Verna's Beemer made it okay as the car roared toward them and the sudden chirp of locked-up brakes on the asphalt.

Verna pulled a couple of emergency blankets from the trunk: the first went over Marcus' shivering form, the second in the car to protect the leather.

Marcus reached out a bloodied hand as they lay him into the clean scent of fine upholstery.

"Keith...Get him out...Yellow Fang nailed us near

Longfellow Bridge…headed southwest along the Esplanade. And Lana—"

"Yes?"

"He's my baby brother."

"No way! You shoulda told me. We'd have dragged him clear before…Shit!" She squeezed his good shoulder for a moment as a promise then slid back out of the car.

"Verna. Pop. You get him to the hospital. He's a good kid. Take care of him."

"No!" Verna cried out and grabbed her arm. "I need you, Lana. Let this one go. Call the cops. Do something else."

She pulled Lana against her. Verna, who never needed anyone, needed her for reasons she'd been trying to fathom for the last several years. She squeezed her so tightly that she could feel the breath huff out of her lover into the chill night.

"It's personal, Verna. It has to be me."

Pop was looking right at her, shaking his head.

"Call the Force."

She turned The Judge by the shoulders and gave her a push toward the car before turning to face her father.

"You don't know the streets anymore, Pop. It's been a pretty wild decade since you retired. Cops roll in and Keith is tomorrow's John Doe DOA. Now get in the car and get out of here. I've got work to do."

Verna dropped the car into gear and her father swung the passenger door shut. He pushed the back door closed with his fingertips, stood up, and faced Lana squarely.

"Let's get going." He waved the BMW off the curb. Verna hesitated only a second then was gone.

"Shit, I don't need an old man on this one."

"This old man can still dance around you. If you wanted to be a cop, why didn't you just stay one? Three years. You quit the week after I retired and now you're playing vigilante living with some fancy pants judge. A damned woman!"

She swung at him. All the shit she'd taken over the years. All the crap she'd worked through that he had dumped on her, year in and year out, that was fine. This was 2003. But if he had the goddamn nerve to say one word about—

He caught her wrist inches from his face. In perfect balance, they struggled. His gray crew-cut made her forget that he still went to the cop's gym and the shooting range five days a week in Florida. He might be retired, but he hadn't stopped being Force by any means.

"I don't have time for this shit." She jerked her hand loose and turned for the Harley. The helmets were upstairs, but she didn't have time for that either.

Lana swung a leg over and rammed her thumb down on the starter. Birds in the nearby trees screamed in protest at being jerked from sleep by the bike's thundering roar. As she knocked back the kickstand her father slid in behind her smelling of Italian spaghetti sauce and Old Spice. There was a smell she'd never forget. That was an instant strikeout on a date for her.

She opened the throttle and roared down the sidewalk letting late night strollers dodge arm-in-arm until she reached the next gap in the parked cars and jounced onto the street.

Cracking the throttle wide cleared three yellow lights be very stale margins, even by Boston standards, but she got through clean. She jogged a block left, her eyes watering as the cold air whipped at her face.

A rough hand from behind pulled open her collar and jammed a fistful of hair down the back of her jacket. It must have been whipping across his face in the speed-driven wind. The slap that pushed her jacket back into place nearly sent them careening into the parked cars.

She jumped the curb and rolled into the Boston

Esplanade—the riverfront park that ran a mile along the Charles River.

Nothing. All quiet.

It had closed hours before so the cop patrol level was way down. There were only a few lights, joggers with warning beacons announcing, "Please come rob my sports watch and iPod." Though why people dropped five hundred bucks on one of the things was beyond her.

Idiots.

There were a lot fewer joggers since the Yellow Fang tong had arrived from Hong Kong. Not because the tong attacked in the parks, but because the other gangs had to push out into less profitable areas like robbery to break even. The tong used strong-arm tactics like the Boston streets had never seen.

A loop around the Hatch bandshell, and still nothing. She just managed to squeeze the wide Harley lay-down bars between the steel posts guarding the Arthur Fiedler Footbridge. She eased up to the top of the ramp and let the bike coast to a stop directly over Storrow Drive.

She killed the engine, though there was no way to hear its gentle throb over the traffic noise. The Back Bay of Boston was traced out in light about them. In the distance, the bright towers of the financial district rose off to the left. Behind them, across the dark strip of the Charles River, Cambridge and half a jillion students hung around MIT and Harvard. To the right was Storrow South and the rest of Commonwealth Ave. Straight ahead lay the Commons, the Gardens, and, on the far side, the Government Center that had once been the Combat Zone—the old source of most of Boston's evil. Now that they'd leveled and rebuilt it, the source was more scattered, harder to trace.

"Why'd we come up here?"

She'd almost forgotten about her father.

"I'm thinking."

"A kid's dying, maybe his brother too and you're busy thinking? How about doing some looking, some asking?"

She twisted to face him as well as she could. "Listen, old man. And after that if you have nothing useful to say, shut the hell up." She stretched an arm out toward the area around the old Zone, indicating sections as she described them.

"There are now five main gangs there, Puerto Rican and Italian with heavy, heavy New York armor to back 'em up. Blacks: small, tough, under-armed. They do the cleanup stuff around the edges: a little numbers, low-grade Colombian. Marcus' old group is called 'FI' as in Fighting Irish."

"The kid said Yellow Fang."

"Yellow Fang is something different. Okay, quick history lesson. You retired in '93. Scroll ahead to 1999, Hong Kong goes back to the People's Republic. Smart, capitalist money doesn't trust the Communists and bails; they buy their way out. Poor folks squat in fishing boats and most of them drown. The tongs—the Chinese gangs—fight their way out. Millions of dollars collected from thousands of sources land the tongs in US and Canadian cities. Red Leopard in New York. Blue Eagle in Chicago. Yellow Fang here. And these guys are into vicious shit. When was the last time you heard of a Zone gang dropping a badge?"

He barely has to blink, "My last year. Kenny O'Malley, patrol second grade. May, 1993. First in six years. And we made them pay on that one."

There was certainly nothing wrong with his memory. It was just out of date.

"Wrong by seven…all in the last three years. All near the Zone. All Yellow Fang. None fatal, six were very close range, and three will never walk again." She knew Pop would understand that very close range meant under two feet so that the powder burns would mark the skin even through their clothes. Those weren't surprise attacks. The officer was already subdued when the trademark hip-shattering trigger was pulled.

"The Italians are holding on, the Puerto Ricans keep sending up more armor but they're losing people six-to-one. Did you ever hear of a ratio like that?"

He was silent.

She looked back at his face.

"Well?"

Finally reluctantly he shook his head. "And you, Lanalee Patterson, all on your own are going to take them on?"

"I'm going to save one kid's life. That's how I do it. One at a time. It's the best I know how and it's what I'd be doing if it weren't for you."

"Without me, you're going to be dead." The arrogance of the man appalled her. She made a mental note of yet another way she would never be like him.

Lana turned back to the city. The chill breeze riding down from the Berkshires ran off the Charles and dropped the temperature across the whole Back Bay. Not many were stupid enough to go into the Commons or Gardens at night —they were even more dangerous than the Esplanade. Locals only went in during heavily-patrolled summer-event nights. But on this cold September night the park was dark. The massive patrols necessary to keep the crowds at least relatively safe were nowhere to be seen. This was normally her favorite time of day. City cozying down for night. Finishing meals and movies, another day done, another to come.

But not the gangs. They'd normally run another couple of hours, moving drugs, working hookers, jacking the odd car.

That's all the time she had. Christ she hoped Verna was safe somewhere among the lights below. She tried to pick out the blue light of Mass General Hospital, but it eluded her. It was going to take some explaining why she hadn't told Pop about Verna for three years, but they'd get it straightened around. She'd been stupid before. Verna was used to that at least.

CHAPTER 5

Judge Verna Carlisle was not about to be denied.

Marcus was unconscious when they arrived; his skin was as white as a sheet of paper, as bloodless as his jacket was bloody. She blew through any paperwork and questions about insurance. Two minutes from arrival to OR. They promised steady reports.

And protection. Two uniformed officers now flanked the door, she could see them posted down the hall. They didn't look one bit happy about pulling guard duty on a Friday night, but Marcus was her only link to Lana at the moment. That was one thing she was absolutely going to protect. Verna needed Lana back in one piece so that she could flay the woman personally.

Suddenly thrown against the wall of inactivity, all she could do was pace from the yellow, cracked, fake leather chairs, past the potted plastic fern to the OR hall door, and back.

Blast Lana for not mentioning their relationship to her father.

But was that why she was so angry? Used to dissecting

the most complex court cases with the cool, passionless rules of the law, she should be able to do the same with her own emotions.

She controlled her shuddering breath and collapsed into the least worn of the chairs. Next time she had her hands on Lana she'd lock her away in a cell to keep her safe. Or give up and toss her back onto the street and let her live out her death wish.

Why was it all so difficult?

Was she angry at Lana for not feeling she was important enough to mention to her father?

Or for not being strong enough to tell him no matter how hard it was?

She closed her eyes and pictured her own father. Judge Carlisle was an honored man in Rutland. Little League coach, always planted the first tree on Arbor Day, first to make a fool of himself on fundraiser talent nights, first to tap the maple trees towering around their house for their sweet sap in the chill of early spring, and the best storyteller as the locals gathered to wait for the sap to sugar down.

He'd taught her law at the dinner table on the cool Vermont evenings. Her mother still had the bookstore that people drove from far and wide to visit. Sometimes they had fights, but not often. And, after the initial shock—done in person the first time she'd been able to convince Lana to go —they'd welcomed Lana as family.

It had been that wild combination of tough and tender that had swept Verna's feet out from under her. Every child or beaten-wife victim that Lana had testified on behalf of in court, their bruises had echoed: the ones on the victim's body and the ones so clear in Lana's eyes. Sky-blue eyes that clouded with internal mists until Verna hadn't been able to look away.

And Lana had wept in her arms the night after she'd met

Verna's parents as a couple. Wept like someone had broken her heart open and the sorrows of the ages had poured out. They almost never spoke of those tearful hours in the darkened farmhouse—only rarely, with the softest of words, after making particularly gentle love. And Lana hadn't cried before or since.

Who the hell was she to judge Lana's life?

Verna hung her head. Curse the woman. She couldn't even stay angry at her.

"Hey, lady. Er…Excuse me."

She looked up at the rangy youth in a white lab tech's smock. His black jeans and red Converse sneakers seemed a bit out of place. She'd never wondered what people wore beneath their hospital coats before. Should have—it was common knowledge in the chambers that Judge Weinstein wore a Bermuda shirt under his robes and that Judge Lacey wore nothing at all under hers.

"That your BMW? Can you move it over to the parking lot?"

She couldn't even remember where she'd parked it, probably left it right at the emergency curb.

"Sure."

She grabbed her purse and headed for the door.

The intern or whatever followed a little ways behind as if people couldn't be trusted to do even that.

CHAPTER 6

*L*ana released the brake and, with a kick off the concrete, rolled silently down the city side of the footbridge. A moment later a high, thin whine passed behind them with a crack that sounded clear above the heavy, night-time traffic.

She punched the starter and nearly pulled a wheelie—despite the massive weight of the bike—when she popped the clutch and cranked open the throttle.

"Hang on, Pop," she shouted back into the wind as another bullet passed right between them. She'd been right about one thing. Yellow Fang were headed back toward Southie where they'd been making the Fighting Irish's lives hell. If they got there, Keith was a goner, because if she followed them that far, she'd never get out herself.

At fifty miles an hour, she could only point and pray as they flew between the metal posts keeping motorized traffic off the walkway.

Clear, they shot out across the Beacon-Arlington intersection, weaving through the traffic. She laid the bike as hard into the corner, skidding on the brick sidewalk, before ramming the front tire square into the low iron gate a hundred feet along Beacon and racing into the cover in the park. Thankfully it hadn't rained in a while and the ground held, but the big bike was getting sloppy anyway. She fought it upright when it tried to pitch them off and reached the first of the oaks.

Killing the engine, she stopped with the tree between them and the direction of the fire, at least as well as she could guess where it was.

Pop was off the bike with his gun out before she could even signal him to do so. Her heel jarred the ground a little sooner than she expected when she got off. A quick nudge with her foot confirmed it. They say you never hear the shot that gets you. The rear tire was flat as a pancake—the bullet had passed right under their butts.

She'd sure miscalculated one thing: how aggressive the gang was tonight. Usually she had a "free pass" from all of the gangs. Sometimes it was less honored, rather than more, but it was rare for someone to take a shot at her. Unless—

Lana had a nasty thought and did her best to discard it. Didn't work any better than shedding her father.

Unless tonight wasn't about Marcus and Keith, but instead about her. She'd taken down a couple of Yellow Fang shooters last week—landed them in hard time for a carjack gone wrong that had orphaned a German kid and also landed the kid in the hospital with two bullets in her gut.

Didn't change the equation. They could do whatever they wanted. She was making tonight about Keith.

And now the silence.

The park had long since emptied. And nothing moved.

Lana reached under the seat being careful not to scorch herself on the exhaust manifold and pulled the Glock and three extra magazines out of their clips. She hated the thing.

She had done three years on the Force—which had given her far too many reasons to use it. She'd always had a nose that led her unerringly into the worst situations. Yeah, she and Maximillian—partners in disaster. That problem hadn't abated when she'd gone private and hired herself on the behalf of the kids.

It was like chance had it in for her. As a PI the confrontations were still messy, but usually a fist or even showing a knife calmed down most of what she ran into. Yellow Fang didn't care crap about knives.

Her pop's nightly debriefing of his day over dinner had taught her how to survive on the streets, but it didn't make it any more fun. In the beginning, her good figure and young face had placed her undercover as a plant in the gangs, or at the schools more often than not.

And she'd drawn the very worst of the scum, both on the streets and on the Force. Which was worse? The ones who wanted to kill her for trying to arrest them or the cops who wanted to fuck her against her wishes in the back of the evidence room? The latter had come out in droves the week after Pop had retired and gone south—as if all the worst of them thought that he'd been the only thing protecting her. A lot of assholes found out the hard way that she could take care of herself—but she'd spent more time in disciplinary hearings than on the job. The battles to clear her name each time had been intense because, of course, it was always the woman's fault.

The day she'd given up and quit was the day she'd had nothing to say to Pop. It had taken her over a year of awkward phone calls to figure out. All they'd ever had to talk about was their work.

She'd quit—and what little there'd ever been of their relationship had never recovered.

"What's going on here?" Pop's voice was steady as a rock.

It was a rare night on the Force to pull your weapon once, never mind twice. And bullets winging by your ear unnerved the most veteran of officers. But not Pop. That would require having feelings.

She slid the spare magazines into her back pockets, and shoved the Glock into her belt. Her usual leathers had a custom holster that normally served as a floppy pocket for her gloves, but those pants were now jammed away under her side of the bed. She'd found dark blue cords and a red silk blouse set out in the bathroom. She took the hint. Thankfully the suede jacket she'd grabbed against the autumn night hid most of the shining fabric Verna had picked out for her.

Lana kicked her mind into gear and set to figuring it out while she scanned the park for movement.

"Someone knew my bike. Must have assumed you were Marcus."

"You were set up."

"No shit. And when I find out who did it, he's going to need a kidney donation, real bad." Lana edged around the tree and ran low toward The Good Samaritan monument because irony was her life and that's where the shot had come from.

Pop slammed into the back of the tree next to her before peering around the edge, his weapon aimed at the sky.

"Did you notice the muzzle flash?"

She took his silence as a negative. She'd seen the second one clearly as she'd kicked the bike to life.

"Rifle."

"Crap." Cops hated rifles in others' hands. You couldn't cruise the streets with a rifle tucked into your back pocket. Rifles meant both planning and ambush.

"How did they know?"

"Because they knew Marcus would run for me, that's why they didn't finish the job and then took his brother."

Another tree and still no sign of movement ahead.

"Yellow Fang likes the Garden when it really wants to make an example of someone. Spread enough guts around and even if the crews find them first, they can't hide it from the early joggers."

"Bastards."

"It's never pretty. But they knew that I knew their reputation."

"What the hell are you doing? *Are* you vigilante?" The foulest curse on the Force dripped with bile from his lips.

She'd asked herself that a thousand times and Verna had echoed her concerns more than once. She hadn't fired her piece outside a range or competition since she'd left the Force. And she'd only pulled the damn thing twice.

Her knife had always been a sufficient threat.

And, mostly, she talked.

She spent hours in grimy coffee shops and hanging out in the dark corners of closed parks. Sometimes a paying client even came her way, usually spousal surveillance or similar crap but it kept her from being a total leech off Verna. Sometimes her share of the expenses had to float a month or so, but she'd always managed to keep her end up.

"No, Pop. I'm not some idiot twenty-year old. I just liked working with the kids. When I was on the Force, my job was more about taking them down and locking 'em away. They deserve better. Now I work to get 'em off the street and back on their feet."

A crack of fire sounded from the darkness where a paved path twisted beneath the shadow of the path they'd just crossed. A flash and a roar behind them knocked her against the tree. She rolled into the tree's sudden shadow cast by the inferno that had been her bike. Her Harley! They were going to pay for that too. Big time! Pop dropped three shots into the darkness.

Lana rose to a low squat and sprinted away. She glanced back and saw that Pop hadn't moved. He still lay on the open grass, his head raised and scanning as he double-handed his revolver in front of him.

She circled back and knocked him aside with a diving roll. Two shots thudded into the soil where he'd lain a moment before. She dragged him behind a tree and slammed him hard enough against the trunk to make his head spin a little.

"Damn it, Pop. Since when do you lay still behind your own muzzle flash. Hunh?"

He opened his mouth and closed it again.

"The shooter knew right where you were. And that shot means there are two of them at least. Now will you just lay low for a moment?"

"Must be out of practice," he rumbled to himself.

Out of practice? He was a seventy-five year old retiree. She didn't know whether to give him a break or tie him up and leave him where he was for his own safety.

She didn't wait to decide, but ran wide, hugging the fence along Arlington. She curved around the burning bike and the flame-engulfed oak which would bring firefighters and police in just minutes, scattering her quarry to the winds.

The fire was intense enough that the heat reached her even beyond the light as she dodged through the flickering shadows. Streetlights washed over the fence illuminating this strip of the park, but it was a chance worth taking.

At a flat-out sprint she had to lean into the twisting jogging path as it cut toward the park. The shooter was sitting exactly where she expected, right near the foot of the monument, using the back of a park bench as a rifle prop.

Too intent on scanning the world before him.

She laid her shoulder low and slammed into his back. The rifle flew clear as she crushed him against the park bench. She rolled clear. He flopped back and groaned. With any luck, she'd broken a couple of ribs, maybe even an arm.

She jumped to her feet, but no such luck, he was just a winded, Asian teen. She grabbed a fistful of hair and controlled him with a sharp twist that elicited a yelp as she patted him down. Two automatics and three knives joined her arsenal. Two more clips for the rifle rested on the bench.

Pop puffed up behind her, and staggered to a halt gasping for breath. He inspected the array of gear and wheezed as he bent to retrieve the rifle.

"This isn't gang stuff. This is a war."

"Sorry, Pop. Except for the nasty piece of gear in your hand, this is pretty mild these days." She fished in her pocket for one of the zip ties she always carried and twisted the kid's arms behind him. She slid up the kid's sleeve to make sure. Yellow hell-dog with bared fangs tattoo right on the forearm as it should be. She jerked one hand through the curved wrought-iron arm of the bench and zipped his wrists together. She wrapped his bandana over his mouth as a quick gag.

Jerking the rifle from Pop's hands, she swung it, with all her might, muzzle down into the dirt.

It sank in a satisfying distance. Plugged. Good and hard.

She jerked it free and swung the butt down hard on the shooter's knee.

A sickening crunch accompanied his muffled scream— now she was sure he wasn't going to be following.

Lana tossed the rifle down beside the bench.

"They think they're safe from this angle. They probably don't know we've taken this shooter out." She gave Pop the chance, but he didn't correct her. She'd done it without his blasted interference. She thought about the hole in her tire and the angle of attack that had required. "The other shooter was east."

The distant whine of sirens now added to the distractions as she worked back toward Beacon Street with Pop in tow. With any luck, she could deal with the gang here in the Gardens without splashing over into the Commons.

Flickers of movement tempted her, but they were too far away to be sure.

Twice she pulled Pop to a halt and waited kneeling in the rhododendrons. The bark chips itching through her thin corduroys as the first of the fire engines pulled up alongside the flaming torch of her bike that lit the night sky. Just through the fence she heard no roar of Friday night traffic. A quick peek confirmed her fears. The traffic had ground to a halt on both major drags with rubberneckers.

And the firefighters had no way of knowing they were in a hot LZ. They would be too tempting a target to this gang gone mad with the bloodlust of the night. She needed to keep moving east and make sure that Yellow Fang went with her to get the rescue workers in the clear.

She bolted from the bushes and sprinted out in the open.

Pop's shout reached out from somewhere behind her.

Weaving from side-to-side she heard two…three bullets wing by.

Two ricocheted off the concrete

The third shattered glass a little farther off.

The accompanying scream sounded more of panic than pain, so she ignored it and kept moving. Too bad rubberneckers never learned their lessons—paybacks were hell.

The gunfire shifted with her, the shadows running on the far side of the clearing, closer to the lake. The center of the Boston Gardens had a lake two football fields long and one wide. Lots of benches, shoreline paths, and shade trees lined its edges. A small footbridge arched high above the pinched middle that almost made it into two lakes.

She dove behind a concrete garbage can and checked the park behind her. The firemen crouched behind their vehicle ignoring the remains of her Harley and the flaming oak. Damn, but she was going to miss that bike.

A spattering of bullets chipped concrete off either side of the garbage can. The solid thud of Pop's revolver repeated through all six chambers and the rain of bullets in her direction ceased.

As fire directed back at the old man, she leapt and bolted into the woods. Two wild shots from the Glock might have distracted their aim. She was safely into a small grove of maples. Now, in darkest shadow, she moved toward them, thanking the park department for how carefully they'd raked up every fallen leaf that might have rustled with her passage.

Moving between two of the trees, she could see the fire truck by her bike with a fireman or two peeking around the edge. Things must have quieted down, for them at least.

Good.

She'd drawn the tong's attention away. At least something had gone right since her father's arrival. Now if she could square things with Verna before they went to sleep tonight that would be nice.

An exploratory shot snapped its way through the leaves thirty feet to her left like an overeager mosquito.

Living through the night was also a good goal.

A bright flash from the rear, toward The Good Samaritan monument, followed a moment later by a loud report. Police training 101, never attempt to use a weapon you don't know the condition of—strike another Yellow Fang member off the list. He'd be pretty banged up if he lived after the explosion of the plugged rifle barrel. The firemen were gone from sight again as the first squad cars began sweeping about the park with their searchlights flickering through the trees. All of them too far away to help.

Or interfere.

Just go to them, Pop.

She scanned behind to see how he was doing just as he bolted into the trees behind her.

Damn.

She whistled and he huffed his way up to her.

"I'm getting too old for this shit."

"Pop, you were at a desk for a decade before you quit. And that was a long time ago."

It was the wrong thing to say. Even before she'd said it, she knew it was the wrong thing. So why did she have to dig at him? She could have sent him back to bring the Force up to date. But no! She'd gone and—

"The hell you say, little girl. You'd be dead if I weren't covering your ass."

When she needed the soft-spoken father who laughed with Verna, she'd gotten the career street cop glaring back at her.

"I'm taller than you are. Little, indeed. And I've had more time on the streets in the last twelve years than you did in the last thirty."

The glare glinted darker in the shadows of the night.

Real smooth, Lana. Real fuckin' smooth.

A squad car searchlight swept by. Nothing moved. It swept back and no figures flickered through the opposite trees.

"Damn. Where'd they go?"

She bolted from the trees and headed south toward the lake. Pop's footsteps thudded along behind her. The searchlight continued to sweep the park in the feeble distance.

One-and-one, she-and-Pop; they skipped ahead, ducked

and held cover, while the other trotted by up on the balls of aching feet.

Elm trees.

Cute boxwood hedges.

More wrought iron benches.

A flurry of swans by the lake.

CHAPTER 7

Despite the gag and blindfold, it was impossible for Verna to mistake where she was. She and Lana had ridden on the swan boats since they were little kids. Probably met there half-a-dozen times without knowing or caring. She was five years older. Back then she would have ignored the little girl, so much younger. Now it just made her the older partner. The one creeping up on the big change. Menopause looming its ugly head. About time all that monthly bother was ended. Why her sister hadn't welcomed it with open arms and a celebration at the Four Seasons was beyond her.

Even if she had noticed the younger Lana, it would only have been to see the bright eyes and easy smile. Of course, that never fit Verna's face when she tried it on in the mirror. At home. With the door locked. But coming up fast on forty, her reflection often smiled. Especially when Lana was around.

Not now.

A shiver she'd been fighting forever—"for half-an-hour at most" some part of her rational brain reported, "for hours" she compromised—threatened once again to take hold and shake her to pieces.

The moment the cold gun had touched the small of her back all warmth had left her body. The boy with the wrong kind of jeans and shoes under a hospital intern's jacket—now she knew how it felt to be stupid. Lana was always trying to protect her, insisting that she didn't want Verna involved in her escapades except from the bench. She'd actually felt a small thrill earlier tonight—beneath the horror—at finally being involved.

Now she was tied to the slat seat of a swan boat pushed into the middle of the Boston Gardens lake on a chilly September night. If something didn't change soon she'd scream. Gagged or not.

Her heart, pounding loud enough to call a SWAT team without a cell phone, insisted on just beating its alarm on the inside of her ears. Only *she* was deafened by her adrenaline's cry for help.

Backfires she'd thought at first.

But they'd moved closer.

Too sharp. Too crisp.

Gunshots.

She was floating in her own little white-swan world while there was a gun battle going on.

Maybe it would wash over her like a wave and brush her quietly under. Judge Verna Carlisle would just become another one of those unknown bodies that were fished from the bottom mud of the pond when they did their routine dredging. Discarded weapons, girl's doll, old beer bottle, judge's body, sunglasses, a bottle of tanning cream. Yeah, pretty typical haul.

A rush of protesting swans filled the air and they flapped and complained their way to the far side of the pond.

Someone was coming. Another shot, loud enough that she'd have screamed in surprise…if she could.

Then silence, an echoing, aching, unending silence.

Lana was out in that silence. Her father too.

Verna's heart slowed down knowing they were coming for her. But no, they didn't know. How could they know? They thought she was sitting safe in a hospital waiting room with two policemen on guard a dozen steps away.

She wasn't about to be rescued.

She was bait.

CHAPTER 8

*L*ana lay beside her father in the slight swale above the lake and scanned the horizon. The fresh-mown grass was sharp in her nose and even covered the usual stench of the swan shit they were probably lying in. The red silk blouse was definitely a write-off. Verna was going to be some kind of angry, it had been a birthday present that she'd always loved. It was amazing how The Judge saw her, feminine and beautiful. Lana would do anything for her.

Through the thin corduroys, the dew was trying to chill her to a slow popsicle. She tried to remember what her Pop was wearing, but couldn't picture anything special. Probably the standard blue jeans and walking shoes he'd worn ever since retirement. Not one of his three precious suits, she was fairly sure.

Except for the wild shot from the north shore, it had been quiet for almost five minutes. The squad cars down by the fire must not have heard it. Though they were sure to be questioning the two gang members by The Good Samaritan. One wouldn't say anything; probably not even if someone did just accidentally happen to sit on the shattered knee. His buddy would either be down or dead depending on how he'd been holding the rifle when it self-destructed as the round blew up in the chamber.

But this wasn't helping them now. The moonlight was weak at best, a bare crescent ducking in and out of clouds. The park's few lights on this side of the closed gates cast dense crisscrossing shadows making hiding easy and movement dangerous.

At a tap on her shoulder, Lana turned to see her father pointing an arm. She followed the finger and spotted the swan boat. It was drifting clear of one of the shadows striking across the water. The others were all tied on the far shore, but this one sat alone in the middle.

There was one…no, two figures aboard. She squinted her eyes and held her breath as the boat turned ever so slowly in the gentle night breeze.

The first swung into view.

In the back seat.

Sitting upright.

With hands crossed in its lap…No. A headless corpse holding it own head in its lap.

Lana turned her head and groaned.

Keith. It had to be Keith. Sorry, Marcus. She had a new mission now. She was personally going to erase these guys from the face of the planet.

She became aware of a string of audible curses next to her.

"Shush, Pop. We've both seen worse."

"It's not that." He pointed again.

The boat had finished turning into the light. Sitting perfectly upright in the front of the boat was a woman.

Lana felt her eyes slide shut and reopen as if she were a sunset fading slowly into the night.

A beautiful woman with shoulder-length dark hair, a

blindfold, and a gag. Dressed in a blue pantsuit. A rumpled, powder-blue pantsuit.

A brutal blow on her back hammered her down into the dirt before she was even aware of jolting to her feet. A few shots zipped by just over their heads—where her head had just been. Without her father there, she'd have done exactly as Yellow Fang had been hoping. Leaped to the rescue and died then and there.

"She's bait, Lanalee. The only way you can help her is to win this thing."

She lay her head down against the grass. Twisted to peek one eye over the edge of the swale. Verna spun quietly, calmly in the middle of the lake like a queen on her throne. Her hands and feet were duct-taped together in front of her.

Lana would die without her.

She closed her eye.

Then opened it and looked again.

Verna was now face on, lit by a floodlamp somewhere behind them. So serene on her throne.

"Hang on, honey," she whispered to the grass. "Lana's comin' for ya', babe. Lana's comin'."

She turned to crawl farther north and her right shoulder hurt like hell where Pop had battered it with his fist.

Damn Pop for being right. He *had* just saved her life.

Her father belly-crawled right along beside her, working farther from the pond as they moved along a line of shadow.

"I'm not leaving you, honey. Lana's coming back. I promise."

A touch on her arm brought her to a stop.

"What do you think, one more shooter or two?"

She considered for a moment. "Second rifle is off to the left facing the pond, near the footbridge that crosses above the middle of the lake. Two pistols to the left. Two rookies on lookout with a knife or something, because they wouldn't trust them with more—get them bloodied a bit in their first big fight. No great loss if they go down. One leader, probably with the rifleman. We got two down and they like to move in groups of eight. Lucky number for Chinese. Leaves six."

And Lana knew, hard cold fact, it was all her fault.

"Must have been squeezing them harder than I thought. They're using their top people if they got Marcus and Keith and knew to go after Verna. Cut them out and we set Yellow Fang way back on its ass."

"Too many, Lanalee. Just too damn many. We need to slide out and get a team in here."

"What the hell?" She scanned the situation quickly from their shadowed conference.

Everything still in place. Verna still spinning slowly in the middle of the lake.

"That's Verna out there." The bile rose until it nearly choked her.

"I know. But there's no way that we two can do all that. I only brought three full loads and I've already used up a set."

"If we need twelve bullets between us to drop these assholes, then we are some sad excuses for truth and justice."

"But there's no way."

Lana tasted it on her tongue…

An idea that was almost formed…

Almost there…

Pop was scared. The old man, with seventy-five good years behind him, was more scared of death than she was.

No.

Too simple. She knew he was too tough to give up on that account.

He was scared by the odds. Well, so was she, but not enough to risk Verna.

What if it had been reversed and his lover was out there, or even a stranger? She'd still go in. Not because she lived more dangerously, though she'd been in nearly as deep a couple times. Pop had never dealt with gangs.

Gang members?

Yes.

Gangs?

No. At least not like this one.

She had to think about this later, but she felt suddenly strong and powerful.

It was so wrong, but it was right as well.

No matter how he had pushed and prodded her—made her feel inferior, incompetent, useless both as a rookie on the Force and as his daughter—she was finally better than he was at something. And that was a revelation she didn't have time to consider.

Lana turned quickly, careful not to rise above their slight cover.

"You work your way around the east end behind them. I'm going straight across the lake and flush them out."

"What? You'll be dead before you swim the second stroke." He grabbed her arm in a panic.

She peeled his iron grip off her bicep. It wasn't easy, but she did it.

"Look. You can help me or not. I have a way across. There'll be a police patrol out this way real soon now. When the cops show up, the rifleman will waste Verna and slither away. They can afford to wait for another day to get me, but I can't. Now move your old fat ass."

Lana didn't wait for his response as she crawled, then rose and ran back along the deepest shadow toward the lake.

She kicked off her boots as she ran and made sure the Glock was shoved down into her underwear so she couldn't lose it. The cold metal made her catch her breath even before she slid into the water.

The steel grating of the drain she'd entered beside

instantly removed any ripples she made as she slid deeper. When only her head remained above water, she hyperventilated in the freezing water as well as she could.

A final breath.

Bearings.

She ducked beneath the water.

The silence was so complete Verna wondered if her hearing had gone bad. The geese had gone back to sleep, their complaints for the night were done.

The gangs had forgotten her. Lana hadn't seen her. Didn't need her.

Silence…and she was still alive.

They no longer needed her as bait, not worth their trouble to rescue.

Which meant Lana was dead.

The tears pooled and burned behind the blindfold. They soaked into the fabric and she bowed her head to her knees.

So much life in one body. Such a big heart.

And it was gone.

A choking sob emptied her lungs.

Her chest ached as she struggled to draw in enough air through her nose.

Calm breathing.

Calm breathing or she'd choke to death.

But Lana…

Oh god.

"Don't move," a voice from the grave spoke from somewhere and she froze.

"I know you can't speak. Pop and I are here, but we've got some unfinished business. If I release you, we're both dead in seconds."

Verna turned her head trying to find the sound of Lana's voice. It was…below her. Mixed in with the slight sound of riplles slapping against the boat's metal pontoons.

"I have to go, but when this is done, I'm going to marry you. It may be legal in only your parents' state. May not even count in Massachusetts, but I don't care."

Verna blinked against the blindfold.

Lana had every phobia in the world about commitment, family, and marriage—all rampant no matter how many times they'd discussed it. And now Lana had proposed to her and she couldn't even answer. The world hadn't just moved, it had changed into something else entirely.

"Who knows, maybe I'll even ask Pop to walk us down the aisle. Tap your foot once for yes."

Damn her! Verna wanted to shout to the sky in celebration and was being offered a foot-tap of a consolation prize. Her feet were so numb from the tape and the cold that she couldn't be sure if she still could move but she tried. With all her soul she tried.

"I love you, Judge Verna Carlisle. I'll be back for you. That's a promise."

Rapid breathing lasted for a moment before a brief splash of Lana ducking once more beneath the water heralded the return of the silence.

She strained her ears. She imagined she could hear a slight groan and a gentle splash somewhere far away. The far side of the lake.

Ten heartbeats.

A hundred.

A shot.

Two more. One sharp, the other rounder.

A scream.

A male scream.

A young male scream repeated.

She held her breath and prayed with all the faith she never knew was in her logical soul.

A double shot.

Silence.

The slow rise of sirens.

And a body entering the water in a splashy dive.

Swimming. Fast swimming.

Lana was coming for her.

CHAPTER 10

*L*ana held the blanket tight around Verna's shoulder as they sat on the hood of Jackson's squad car. The warm engine felt good against her butt as someone wrapped a blanket around her, too.

Pop was filling in the rapt patrolmen.

"So I sent Lana into the water. Figured she could catch a breath at the swan boat and keep…"

"Hey! That's not—"

Verna's elbow caught her in the ribs.

She turned to face The Judge. "But he just—"

Verna grabbed the back of her head and smashed their lips together.

Lana tried to argue, but Verna's workouts at the gym gave her a surprising amount of strength for such a slight woman. A strength Lana had enjoyed, reveled in under other circumstances.

But Pop was rewriting history.

As she protested against her lover's lips, she could feel the smile forming there. It bubbled up into laughter.

Verna threw her arms around her neck and whispered into her ear.

"He's never going to change, Lanalee Patterson-Carlisle. You will simply have to accept that."

"But he—" And then the compound name slid home. She was going to marry Verna and make a family of their own devising.

Verna soft lips and strong tongue stopped her thoughts completely.

Maybe they could get away to Vermont this weekend.

She'd deal with Pop later.

ONE CHEF! (EXCERPT)

A DEAD CHEF FOODIE THRILLER

$\mathcal{M}$arianne Rimaldi scooped a scant teaspoon of the Gran Marnier chocolate ganache and drizzled it atop the single bite of truffle cheesecake. The perfect final bite for the meal she was creating.

A glance at the competition clock.

Two minutes.

She plated three more desserts for the judges. The television cameras filming *Kate's Kitchen from Hell* hovered close by—two on her, two on her competitor as the final seconds ticked away. One glass-eyed lens had an angle that showed the cameraman wasn't focused only on the food.

Precisely according to plan.

Marianne needed the win on America's most popular cooking show, which meant winning over at least two judges. More than that, she lusted after that *Kate's Kitchen* "Golden Knife" stamp of approval on her career, which required all three judges. For that she wasn't above applying other…ingredients.

The heat of the competition kitchen—the flaring burners and blinding stage lights—had "forced" her to undo the cross-shoulder buttons of her confining chef's jacket which now hung half open. She wore a loose-necked satin blouse beneath, no bra. She'd chosen a emerald green to contrast with the fire-red of the winner's jacket that she hoped to be awarded at the end of the show. It also stood out well against her unadorned ash-black jacket of a contestant, but she wanted the red.

However, mere party tricks wouldn't work on the show's main judge.

Marianne had to capture Kate Stark's attention. With her, nothing would count except the food itself.

Kate Stark, the blue-eyed goddess of television food on the nation's most popular cooking network, was also founder and perennial judge of the show. Always front and center on the final panel.

Deep down Marianne didn't want to just win Stark's vote, she wanted to impress the hell out of her. She'd sell her soul to Devil if needs be; it was *Kate's Kitchen from Hell* after all.

Don't think! Focus on the food...but don't forget the theater.

Marianne was slightly built, so even the least view down her blouse from above was a very revealing one. She bent over her dessert plates and the satin draped away from her body allowing a deliciously cool ripple to course down her front. Her build might be far less substantial than the one that had made her mother such a success on the "wrong" side of Hollywood. But she'd certainly watched her mom and learned what sold. It had been an educational upbringing, if not a typical one.

Three judges.

Two of them were easy.

The guest taster was Zania in the role of the "every person's" palate so necessary for engaging an audience. Someone for the viewers to identify with, among all those professional chefs. Of course her palate was about the only thing on Zania that wasn't extraordinary.

Zania was the hottest new Hollywood starlet—who Marianne would bet was a closet butch. It wasn't too dangerous a bet because Zania's mother worked the same side of Hollywood as Marianne's and word got around of what really happened after the bedding was rumpled in erotic film.

During her intro, Tinsel Town's hot new box-office draw had announced she was centerfolding for *Playboy* next month in the same sultry breath as promoting her new tight-leather, sci-fi thriller movie. Marianne knew that anyone who pegged Zania as an airhead had a nasty surprise coming; she absolutely knew how to market herself. In all ways.

However, hinting to the actress that there was a chance of some woman-on-woman bonding that would allow Zania to prove just who was the "ultimate female among women" offered real possibilities for leveraging the star's vote. It definitely looked as if she'd bought into Marianne's careful seasoning of her performance with hints and suggestions.

Marianne's own tastes however, were for the second guest judge; the professional chef.

Harold Merritt, with his Michelin-starred *Chicago's Merritt* restaurant, was both very handsome and notoriously single. Win or lose, she'd make a point of chatting him up after the show. All that broad chest and short dark crew cut gave him a deliciously tough look; she could find many uses for him outside the kitchen, or in it—a little oil, two bodies, maybe some chocolate sauce...

A careful peek from behind the screen of the jet-black dyed bangs of her blond hair revealed Zania and Harold were staring hard at their monitors of the show's live feed rather than gazing benignly over the competition kitchen floor. Their attention was right where Marianne wanted it. On her.

The head judge was a different problem.

Kate Stark—the number one slotted television chef on any network, not just the one she owned—also watched the monitor, but with a slightly amused smile that Marianne would pay a lot to understand. Kate with her direct blue eyes and straight brunette hair that brushed her shoulders and framed the well-defined cheekbones and aquiline nose that made her one of the most attractive faces in television, cooking or not.

She was a notoriously deadpan judge, at least on this show, so that wry smile must mean something.

For good or ill, Marianne would not find the answer to that this side of the judge's table.

The camera that was spying down her jacket still hadn't wavered, so Marianne "accidentally" dribbled a large dollop of the orange-chocolate ganache onto the back of her hand. She licked it clean as if too hurried to wipe it away, making sure the camera could see the pleasure on her face at the success of her own work without losing the angle on her blouse.

Damn! It really was good. Marianne would win on taste alone. But she'd have to play the meal presentation very carefully, spiking the odds even further in her favor with both of the two guest judges.

The competition buzzer sounded as she shaved the last of the zest of a blood orange using a nutmeg rasp. Even as Marianne held up her hands to show she was done, the camera focused in on the cloud of orange dust still sprinkling down like the first snowflakes.

Her shiny dark green satin blouse made a perfect backdrop, which had "somehow" slipped out of another button. Somehow…because she'd enlarged the buttonhole last night to ensure that the button popped when she raised her arms.

Nailed it.

She had to close her eyes for a moment to steady herself.

Light-headed.

She needed to eat.

Her normal technique of shrugging it off didn't work. Even lowering her arms and subtly bracing herself against the table didn't help clear her head.

Her hands were shaking.

Her hands never shook.

Franco Lamar cursed.

The damned bitch wasn't supposed to taste her own food, not that big teasing lick off the back of her hand anyway. A small taste and she'd have been fine. For a while. Long enough anyway.

Now he could see Marianne Rimaldi wavering from where he and his men lurked in the shadows of the television studio, far behind the judges' table and well clear of any camera's eye.

Bitch was really pissing him off.

He held his breath, keeping his men in place. He had a Plan B, but he hated when that happened. Especially because he didn't have a Plan C.

Rimaldi made it through the other competitor's meal service by clutching the edge of her work table, rousing herself to high-five her sous chef, but little else.

The studio emptied. Last shoot of the day. Competitor headed for the bathroom after the judges were done critiquing him. All the main kitchen staff and cameramen drifted out just as he'd planned.

Now he was down to three judges, two cameramen, one floor director, and dumb bitch Rimaldi.

She served the first of her three main dishes. Oohs and ahs and cheerful commentary among the sappy judges.

Franco could feel his fingers digging into his opposite arms where they were crossed. He always hated this part the most.

In Marine Force Recon, they'd parachute down behind enemy lines, observe, assess, and report. They could be weeks on the ground playing cat-and-mouse games with enemy security and military forces. That was fine. Even laying low between the final "Go" and the actual zero-hour start of the operation was easy; you found a willing local female, or an unwilling one, and you laid her low until it began.

It was the time between the actual start of the operation and the launch of his role in it that had always eaten at him.

Full alert and on hold sucked. It sucked when he was still in Recon and it sucked now.

Rimaldi was wavering, but fighting it well through the first three plates of her meal. Her body was shutting down on her and she'd have no idea why. Her brain was going with it so she was probably past caring.

C'mon bitch. Just hold it together long enough to deliver the dessert clean.

She almost dumped the final dessert plates to the studio's cement floor, earning gasps of surprise from the judges and cameramen.

But she recovered and made it to the table.

Franco held his breath as she stumbled through her presentation. The drug was allowing so little oxygen to her brain that it was amazing she was still standing.

Done.

Now the tasting.

C'mon judges.

The movie star wench did even better than he could have hoped.

She ate the poisoned dessert in two neat bites. Then the stupid whore picked up her plate to lick up the puddled chocolate sauce with a long, sensuous move.

Licking that plate clean on top of the dessert was a massive overdose, not just a knockout.

She collapsed forward, face down into the plate.

Shit!

Franco looked at the other two judges as the studio exploded in panic.

Kate Stark's hand rested on the male judge's arm to keep him from eating.

The two primary targets both sat there—undrugged.

Rimaldi's body finally figured out that it was already dead and she collapsed to the floor.

That put paid on the two secondary targets: Rimaldi and Zania were past recovery.

Still Stark and the guy sat there unmoving.

Franco nodded to Jason.

Jason Mann pulled out a dart gun and shot them both in the back of the neck.

They each flinched in turn, then slowly collapsed forward.

Available at fine retailers everywhere!

ABOUT THE AUTHOR

M.L. Buchman started the first of, what is now over 50 novels and as many short stories, while flying from South Korea to ride his bicycle across the Australian Outback. Part of a solo around the world trip that ultimately launched his writing career.

All three of his military romantic suspense series—The Night Stalkers, Firehawks, and Delta Force—have had a title named "Top 10 Romance of the Year" by the American Library Association's *Booklist*. NPR and Barnes & Noble have named other titles "Top 5 Romance of the Year." In 2016 he was a finalist for Romance Writers of America prestigious RITA award. He also writes: contemporary romance, thrillers, and fantasy.

Past lives include: years as a project manager, rebuilding and single-handing a fifty-foot sailboat, both flying and jumping out of airplanes, and he has designed and built two houses. He is now making his living as a full-time writer on the Oregon Coast with his beloved wife and is constantly amazed at what you can do with a degree in Geophysics. You may keep up with his writing and receive a free book by subscribing to his newsletter at: www.mlbuchman.com

Join the conversation:
www.mlbuchman.com

Other works by M. L. Buchman:

The Night Stalkers
Main Flight
The Night Is Mine
I Own the Dawn
Wait Until Dark
Take Over at Midnight
Light Up the Night
Bring On the Dusk
By Break of Day
White House Holiday
Daniel's Christmas
Frank's Independence Day
Peter's Christmas
Zachary's Christmas
Roy's Independence Day
Damien's Christmas
and the Navy
Christmas at Steel Beach
Christmas at Peleliu Cove
5E
Target of the Heart
Target Lock on Love
Target of Mine

Firehawks
Main Flight
Pure Heat
Full Blaze
Hot Point
Flash of Fire
Wild Fire
Smokejumpers
Wildfire at Dawn
Wildfire at Larch Creek
Wildfire on the Skagit

Delta Force
Target Engaged
Heart Strike
Wild Justice

White House Protection Force
Off the Leash
On Your Mark
In the Weeds

Where Dreams
Where Dreams are Born
Where Dreams Reside
Where Dreams Are of Christmas
Where Dreams Unfold
Where Dreams Are Written

Eagle Cove
Return to Eagle Cove
Recipe for Eagle Cove
Longing for Eagle Cove
Keepsake for Eagle Cove

Henderson's Ranch
Nathan's Big Sky
Big Sky, Loyal Heart

Love Abroad
Heart of the Cotswolds: England
Path of Love: Cinque Terre, Italy

Dead Chef Thrillers
Swap Out!
One Chef!
Two Chef!

Deities Anonymous
Cookbook from Hell: Reheated
Saviors 101

SF/F Titles
The Nara Reaction
Monk's Maze
the Me and Elsie Chronicles

Strategies for Success (NF)
Managing Your Inner Artist/Writer
Estate Planning for Authors